Shadow Puppets

Diana Noonan
Photography by Alice McBroom

Contents

Puppets

Puppets come in all shapes and sizes.

Shadow Puppets

Shadow puppets are easy to make.

Shadow puppets can be made from paper, wood or cloth. You can even use your hands!

Make a Shadow Puppet with Your Hands

Make a shadow puppet with your hands.

barking dog

See if you can make a barking dog. Move your little finger to open and close the dog's mouth.

You can make a flying bird and a quacking duck, too.

Make a Shadow Puppet on a Straw

Make a shadow puppet using a cut-out shape on a straw.

You will need:

- a drawing of an animal or a person
- scissors
- a straw
- sticky tape.

butterfly

rabbit

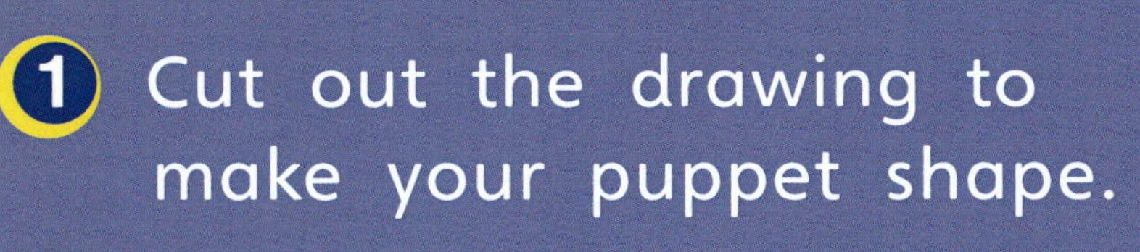

1. Cut out the drawing to make your puppet shape.

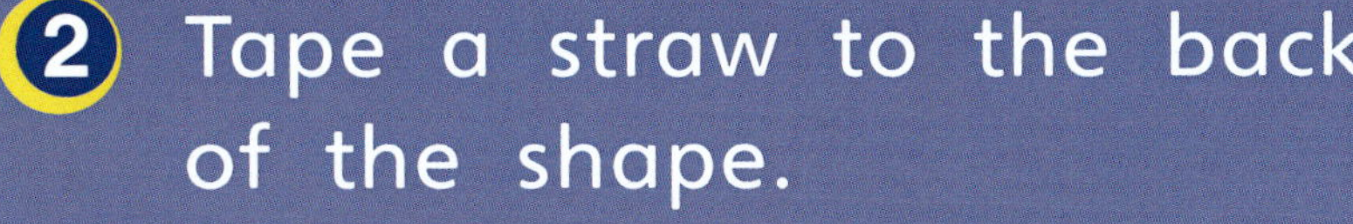

2. Tape a straw to the back of the shape.

Make a shadow with your puppet!

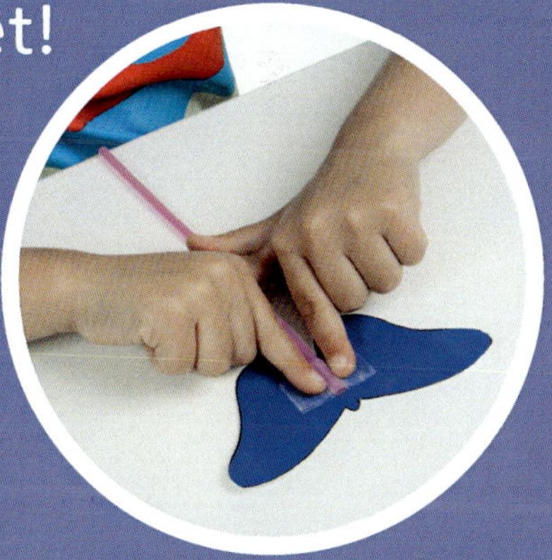

Make a Shadow Puppet with Moving Parts

Make a puppet with moving parts.

Moving parts can be:

- a head that nods
- a hand that waves
- a tail that swishes.

Let's make a horse with a head that nods.

You will need:

- a drawing of a horse's head and body
- card
- scissors
- a paper fastener
- two straws
- sticky tape.

1. Cut out the horse's head and body.
2. Overlap the two parts. Push the paper fastener through the holes. Get an adult to help you.

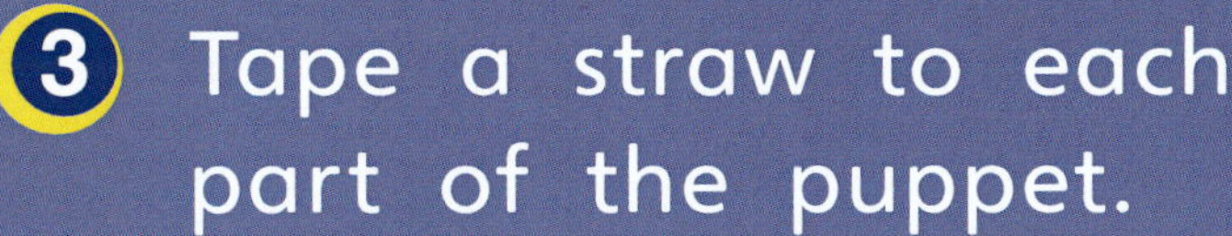

3 Tape a straw to each part of the puppet.

Bring your shadow puppet to life!

Make a Stage

There are different ways to make a stage for your shadow puppets.

1. Use a wall to make shadows with your puppets.
   - Shine a light onto a wall.
   - Hold your puppets in front of the light.

2. Make your own stage using a box.
   - Get an adult to help you cut off the top and bottom of a box.
   - Tape some thin paper on one side of the box. Add some decorations.
   - Shine a light behind the stage.

Lights On!
A light can be a lamp or a torch.

Make Up a Play

Sit behind the stage and hold up your puppets. Practise moving the puppets and making them talk.

Let the Show Begin!

Now you are ready to put on a shadow puppet show. Shine a light behind the puppets – and let the fun begin!

Index